VALENTINE'S DAY

Mrs. Becker announced to the class that they would start making Valentine's Day cards. "I'd like a volunteer to pass out the art supplies," she said.

Jessica raised her hand.

"Jessica, how about you?" Mrs. Becker said. "And please choose someone to help you."

Jessica stood up and looked at Elizabeth. Elizabeth looked at her hopefully. They always did things together. But Jessica looked first at her friend, Lila, and then at Elizabeth's friend, Amy. She knew how to get back at Elizabeth for liking the new girl Eva better.

"Amy can help me," Jessica said.

SWEET VALLEY KIDS

ELIZABETH'S VALENTINE

Created by
FRANCINE PASCAL

Written by
Molly Mia Stewart

Illustrated by
Ying-Hwa Hu

A BANTAM SKYLARK BOOK®
NEW YORK · TORONTO · LONDON · SYDNEY · AUCKLAND

RL 2, 005–008

ELIZABETH'S VALENTINE
A Bantam Skylark Book / February 1990

*Sweet Valley High®, and Sweet Valley Kids are
trademarks of Francine Pascal*

Conceived by Francine Pascal

*Produced by Daniel Weiss Associates, Inc.,
33 West 17th Street
New York, NY 10011*

Cover art by Susan Tang,

*Skylark Books is a registered trademark of Bantam Books, a division of
Bantam Doubleday Dell Publishing Group, Inc.*

ISBN 0-553-15761-2

Published simultaneously in the United States and Canada

*Bantam Books are published by Bantam Books, a division of Bantam Double-
day Dell Publishing Group, Inc. Its trademark, consisting of the words
"Bantam Books" and the portrayal of a rooster, is Registered in U.S. Patent
and Trademark Office and in other countries. Marca Registrada. Bantam
Books, 666 Fifth Avenue, New York, New York 10103.*

PRINTED IN THE UNITED STATES OF AMERICA

OPM   20 19 18 17 16 15 14 13 12

112358

To Taryn Rebecca Adler

CHAPTER 1

Grumpy Jessica

Jessica Wakefield had been in bed with the flu that was going around her class at Sweet Valley Elementary School.

"I hate being sick," Jessica grumbled the moment she woke up. She sat up slowly so she wouldn't feel too dizzy, and swallowed. Her throat didn't feel scratchy the way it did yesterday. And her stomach didn't feel like she was on a roller coaster anymore, either.

Jessica rearranged her stuffed animals and thought of what to say to her mother.

She had already missed three days of school and she didn't want to miss any more.

"Jess?" came a soft voice. Very slowly, the bedroom door opened. Jessica's identical twin sister, Elizabeth, tiptoed in.

"Are you up yet?" Elizabeth whispered. "I have to get my school clothes." She was still in her green pajamas.

Jessica stuck out her lower lip. "I'm awake."

"Do you still feel yucky?" Elizabeth asked. She felt bad for Jessica. Being identical twins meant they were very close to each other. If one of them was happy, the other felt happy, and if one was sad, the other felt sad, too.

The twins shared everything. They sat side by side in Mrs. Becker's second-grade class. They shared toys, and split candy and

treats right down the middle. And usually they shared a bedroom, but Elizabeth was sleeping on the foldaway bed in the den because Jessica was sick.

"I want to go to school today," Jessica said.

"You do?" Elizabeth giggled. "You *never* want to go to school!"

Both girls had long blond hair with bangs and blue-green eyes. They looked exactly alike, but that didn't mean they liked the same things. They were identical on the outside but not on the inside, Elizabeth liked to say. She was the one who liked school and reading. Jessica liked to play with her friends.

"If I don't go to school today," Jessica said, "I might miss making Valentine's Day cards. And I'll definitely miss meeting Eva."

"Oh, that's right," Elizabeth said. She took

4

a pair of jeans and a blue shirt out of her dresser. "This will be Eva's first day in school, and Mrs. Becker will be picking someone to be her host."

"I wanted it to be me," Jessica said, sniffling.

"Maybe Mrs. Becker will wait until you get back," Elizabeth suggested.

Jessica folded her arms. "She'll pick Lila. I just know it."

Eva was a new student in their class. She was coming from Jamaica, one of the islands of the West Indies. Mrs. Becker had shown them where it was on the map. Jamaica was a long way from California, where the twins lived. Lila Fowler, who was Jessica's next-best friend after Elizabeth, had been there once on vacation. Jessica was sure Lila would be picked as Eva's host because of that.

5

"It's just not fair," she complained, as she swung her legs over the edge of her bed. "I hate missing school. It's so boring at home."

Elizabeth looked surprised. "But you get to watch TV all day if you want."

"I know, but most of the shows are for little kids," Jessica grumbled.

"You could read."

Jessica made a face. "I don't want to read books all day long."

Elizabeth thought some more. "You get to eat breakfast and lunch in bed," she pointed out.

"My bed is full of crumbs!" Jessica stood up and marched to her closet. "I'm getting dressed."

"Whoa, young lady!" Mrs. Wakefield came into the bedroom at that moment. She felt

Jessica's forehead. "I don't think you're ready to go back to school just yet," she said.

Jessica sniffled. "But, Mom! I'm all better!"

"No buts," their mother said. "Maybe tomorrow. But right now you're hopping right back into that bed."

Elizabeth gave Jessica a sympathetic smile.

Jessica climbed back into bed. This was the worst time of all to get sick. If she couldn't go to school, someone else would be picked to be Eva's host. And Jessica had a feeling it would be Lila.

CHAPTER 2

The New Girl

Elizabeth sat in her school chair and put her homework on her desk. Jessica's empty seat was next to hers. Elizabeth wished her twin would get better. She felt lonely without her.

"Psst," Lila Fowler whispered. She was on the other side of Jessica's empty desk. "The new girl is coming today!" Lila said. She lifted her chin in the air. "I'm sure I'll get picked to be her host. I've been to Jamaica, you know. No one else in our class has."

Elizabeth nodded without looking up. Lila

was such a show-off. "I know," was all she said.

Everyone else was whispering about the new girl, too. They all wondered what she would be like. Mrs. Becker hadn't arrived yet, but Ricky Capaldo was standing guard by the door.

"Here they come now!" Ricky shouted. He ran to his chair and sat down.

Elizabeth smiled. She was excited about someone coming from so far away. Maybe Eva would become a new friend.

In walked Mrs. Becker with a girl by the hand. Everyone stared at her with great curiosity. Elizabeth thought she was very pretty. Eva had large brown eyes and her hair was in a fluffy ponytail with a ribbon at the top. She smiled shyly, and looked down at the floor.

"Class, this is Eva Simpson," Mrs. Becker said cheerfully. "Let's give her a big hello."

"Hi!" all the kids said at once. Elizabeth wished Eva would look her way. She wanted to welcome the new girl with a big smile.

"Hello," Eva whispered to the class. The way she said it sounded very nice, almost as if she were singing the word. Mrs. Becker had told them she would have an accent that sounded a little bit British.

"Look at her dress," Lila whispered across Jessica's seat. "That's a special Jamaican dress."

Eva was wearing a blue jumper with a white blouse underneath. The outfit looked very neat, but Elizabeth didn't notice anything unusual about it. Lila was just being a know-it-all.

"I think we'll sit you right here," Mrs.

Becker told Eva as she led her to Jessica's empty seat. The rest of the kids turned around in their chairs to watch. "Make yourself at home."

Lila smiled proudly, and Elizabeth felt worried. She hoped Mrs. Becker remembered that this was Jessica's seat. And Jessica had been right—it certainly looked like Mrs. Becker was going to pick Lila. Elizabeth tried not to let it bother her. She looked at Eva and smiled. Eva smiled back.

"Hi," Elizabeth said.

"Hi," Eva said quietly.

"I've been to Jamaica," Lila announced proudly to Eva.

"Now," Mrs. Becker said. "Eva needs someone to show her around school and make her feel at home in her new neighborhood."

Lila nodded and gave Elizabeth an I-told-you-so smile.

Mrs. Becker sat at her desk. "I had a hard time choosing someone," she began. "Since Eva comes from another country, I'm picking the student who got the best marks in social studies this year—Elizabeth."

"What?" Lila gasped.

Elizabeth was surprised and happy and excited at the same time. "That's me!" she said, turning toward Eva. "I'm Elizabeth."

"E for Eva, E for Elizabeth," Eva said. She smiled. "And E for excellent!"

"That's right!" Elizabeth laughed. She could tell they were going to be good friends.

At lunchtime, Elizabeth took Eva through the milk line. Then they sat down together at a table.

"We're sitting with you!" Lila said as she came over with Ellen Riteman and Amy Sutton. Amy was Elizabeth's best friend after Jessica.

"Fine," Elizabeth said. "Eva, this is Lila, Ellen, and Amy," she said as she pointed to the others.

Eva carefully opened her milk. "Hello," she said.

"You have an accent," Ellen said. "Say something long."

Eva thought for a moment. "I know," she said. "Peter Piper picked a peck of pickled peppers."

Lila giggled. "Peta pipa picked a peck of pickled peppas," she said, trying to sound like Eva. "It sounds nicer when you say it."

"Do you always dress up for school?" Ellen asked.

14

"This is my school uniform," Eva replied. "I wore it to my old school but my mother says I can get blue jeans and T-shirts now that we live here."

"What's Jamaica like?" Amy asked. She took a big bite of her tuna sandwich. "Are there sharks in the water?"

Lila scrunched her face. "Don't listen to her, Eva. She's a shark nut."

Eva smiled and nodded. "I like sharks, too. But not when I'm swimming."

Everyone laughed except Lila. "I think sharks are horrible," she said in her snobby way. "Only tomboys like them."

Elizabeth wondered if Lila was angry that she wasn't Eva's host. She was acting a little bit mean to the new girl.

"You think you're so smart, Lila," Amy said. She stuck her tongue out. "So there."

15

Eva looked at Elizabeth nervously.

"They always act that way," Elizabeth whispered to her. "Don't worry."

"OK," Eva whispered back. Her brown eyes looked happy. "I'm glad Mrs. Becker picked you to help me."

"Me, too." Elizabeth couldn't wait to get home to tell Jessica the good news.

CHAPTER 3

Center of Attention

The next morning, Jessica felt well enough to go to school. She was glad she hadn't missed making Valentine's Day cards, but she had missed the new girl's first day. "Do you think Eva will like me?" she asked Elizabeth as they jumped off the bus.

"Of course! She's really nice," Elizabeth answered. They both hurried toward their classroom.

At first, Jessica had been upset that Mrs. Becker had chosen Elizabeth. Then she decided it was almost the same as being picked herself. And it was a lot better than if Lila had been chosen. Now Jessica couldn't wait to meet Eva.

"Will she wear her school uniform again?" Jessica asked.

Elizabeth walked a little faster. "I don't know. Eva said she was going to buy new clothes for school."

They entered the classroom.

"Hi, Jessica!" Lila said, running over. "I hope you don't make me sick."

"I won't," Jessica replied. She stared across the room. The new girl was sitting in *her* chair! Jessica looked at Lila. "She's sitting in my seat."

"That's where Mrs. Becker told her to sit," Lila said. "I guess you'll have to sit somewhere else."

Jessica frowned. Almost all the kids in the

18

class were crowded around Eva. Todd Wilkins was showing her his baseball glove, Amy Sutton was braiding her hair, and the others were asking her lots of questions. Eva said something funny, and everyone laughed, including Elizabeth.

"No one seems to notice I'm back," Jessica said glumly. She thought everyone would be fussing over her, but they weren't. Instead, everyone was busy talking to Eva.

Jessica started pouting. "I want my own seat back."

Lila practiced a dance pose. "I bet Mrs. Becker won't let you have it."

"She'd better," Jessica grumbled. She went up to the teacher's desk and waited.

"Hello, Jessica!" Mrs. Becker said when she finally arrived. She gave Jessica a big smile. "I'm glad you feel better. Welcome back."

"Mrs. Becker?" Jessica said. "Someone is sitting in my seat." She pointed to Eva.

"I wanted her to sit next to Elizabeth," Mrs. Becker explained. "But I know you like to sit next to your sister, too. I have an idea."

Mrs. Becker walked over to the group of kids. "Amy, would you let Eva sit in your seat for a few days?" she asked. Amy's desk was on the other side of Elizabeth's.

"OK," Amy said. She picked up her books and moved to an empty desk. Eva shifted over two seats. She sat on one side of Elizabeth and Jessica sat down in her regular seat on the other.

"Good," Elizabeth said. "Eva, this is Jessica. She's my sister."

"Hello, Jessica," Eva said, smiling. "Elizabeth told me she had a twin sister. I've never met twins before. It must be a lot of fun."

Jessica frowned. "Sometimes," she said. She checked her desk to see if everything was in the right place. She didn't feel very happy that Elizabeth knew Eva so well already.

"OK, class, settle down!" Mrs. Becker began. "First, I want to say that Valentine's Day is next week and that we'll be making cards the day before. So start thinking about what kind of cards you want to make—and who your secret valentine will be this year." She started to write on the blackboard. "Now we're going to learn a little bit about Jamaica and I'd like Eva to help us."

Jessica looked over at her twin. Elizabeth was whispering something to Eva across the aisle. "You give valentines to all the people you like. Everyone makes lot of heart-shaped cards," she heard Elizabeth whisper to Eva. Elizabeth *never* whispered in class when Jessica wanted to!

"Psst!" Lila hissed.

Jessica looked over at her friend. "What?"

Lila pointed at Eva. "She's wearing the same uniform she wore yesterday. Isn't it dumb-looking?"

Jessica looked at Eva's blue jumper. At first she had thought it was pretty, but now she agreed with Lila.

"Yuck," she whispered back. "What a gross outfit."

"I don't like her very much," Lila whispered in Jessica's ear.

"Me, neither," Jessica mumbled. She decided that being back in school was no fun at all.

CHAPTER 4

Left Out

When the girls came down for breakfast on Saturday morning, Mrs. Wakefield was making pancakes.

"Mom! Can we have our pancakes in the shape of animals?" Elizabeth asked. She ran to the stove and looked into the frying pan. Mrs. Wakefield was very artistic and Elizabeth thought she could do almost anything.

Her mother laughed. "OK. Animal pancakes coming up."

Pretty soon, Elizabeth and Jessica each had a stack of pancakes that looked like fat, round cows, and rabbits with large heads and long ears. Elizabeth dripped syrup over hers and then passed the bottle to her sister.

"Don't forget, Amy is coming over today," Elizabeth said to Jessica. "To go swimming." The Wakefields had an aboveground pool in their backyard.

"I know," Jessica replied.

Elizabeth bit the legs off one pancake. Then she thought of something. "Mom? Can I invite Eva, the new girl over, too?"

"I think that's a very good idea," their mother said. "I'll give her mother a call."

Elizabeth bounced in her seat. "Great. I can't wait."

Jessica didn't say anything.

"But no swimming for you today, Jessica," Mrs. Wakefield said. "It's a little too chilly and I don't want you to get sick again."

Jessica stuck out her lower lip. "I don't care."

Elizabeth wondered why Jessica was in a bad mood. Maybe she was still feeling a little bit sick, Elizabeth thought. Whatever it was, she wished her sister would cheer up.

Elizabeth was already in her bathing suit when Amy arrived. "Do you want to go swimming before we play some games?" Elizabeth asked her.

"Sure. I'm ready," Amy said. She took off her T-shirt and shorts. Underneath was her pink bathing suit. "Let's do cannonballs!"

Elizabeth laughed. "Race you!"

They ran out to the backyard. Mr. Wakefield and Jessica were sitting in lawn chairs. "Hello, Amy," Mr. Wakefield called out. Amy waved to him before she and Elizabeth both jumped into the water.

"AAAAH!" Amy screamed. "It's cold!"

"You'll get used to it," Elizabeth said. She grabbed her inflatable shark and hung onto it. "You know who else is coming over?"

Amy stood at the shallow end. "Who?"

"Eva," Elizabeth said, splashing water toward Amy. "She should be here pretty soon."

Amy smiled. "I'm glad." She took a kickboard off the edge of the pool and started kicking toward the deep end. She didn't know how to swim yet, but she was trying to learn. "Can Eva swim?"

Elizabeth nodded. "She told me her mother said she knew how to swim before she could walk! I'll bet she's really good."

"Elizabeth!" Mrs. Wakefield called. "Eva's here!"

27

"Hooray!" Elizabeth cheered, and climbed up the ladder. Amy followed.

"Hi, Eva," Elizabeth said.

Eva had on a pink two-piece bathing suit with ruffles. "Hi. Thank you for inviting me," she said. "Hello, Amy."

Amy smiled. "Hi. Elizabeth says you already know how to swim?"

"Sure! I can do lots of things in the water!" Eva ran to the pool. "Can you do somersaults?"

Elizabeth's eyes widened. "Do you know how?"

"Watch!" Eva jumped in the air, grabbed her knees, and cannonballed into the water with a big splash. Then she ducked underwater, did a handstand and then a somersault before she popped up again.

"Wow!" Elizabeth clapped her hands. "You're good! Isn't Eva good?" she asked Amy.

Her friend shrugged. "I guess so."

"I want to try what you just did," Elizabeth said. She jumped into the water and walked over to Eva. "Can you teach me?"

Eva nodded. "Can you put your face in the water?"

"Yes," Elizabeth said. She was so excited to be learning water gymnastics that she didn't notice that Amy stayed out of the water.

"I love to swim," Eva said. She floated on her back and swirled the water with her hands. "Isn't it fun?"

Elizabeth smiled. It sure was fun to have a friend who was just like a mermaid! "Show me how to do a somersault."

"OK," Eva said.

For a while, Elizabeth and Eva practiced handstands and somersaults. Elizabeth thought Eva was the best swimmer she knew. She just wished Jessica could be learning with her.

That reminded her about Amy. Elizabeth quickly went to the ladder and climbed up. Amy and Jessica were sitting in the lawn chairs, whispering. They stopped when they saw Elizabeth looking at them.

"Aren't you coming back in?" Elizabeth asked Amy.

Amy shrugged. "Maybe." Then she began talking to Jessica again.

Elizabeth wondered if Amy and Jessica had a secret. Behind her, Eva was splashing like a dolphin.

"Isn't Amy coming in?" Eva said.

"I don't know," Elizabeth answered. She

felt sad all of a sudden, but she didn't know why.

Eva climbed up the ladder, too. Drops of water sparkled on her arms. "Is Amy mad at me?" she asked quietly.

"No!" Elizabeth shook her head. "That's a silly idea."

"Oh. I just wondered," Eva said. She looked down at the grass. Then she looked at Elizabeth with a smile. "Is that your cat?"

Elizabeth was surprised. "What? We don't have a cat."

"I thought I heard a meow," Eva explained. She pointed to some bushes. "Over there."

Together, Elizabeth and Eva climbed down and peeked into the bushes, but they saw nothing.

"What are you guys looking at?" Jessica called.

Elizabeth stood up. "Eva heard something."

Jessica and Amy looked at each other and rolled their eyes. They had a secret, all right. But Elizabeth didn't know what it could be.

CHAPTER 5

Seesaw Friends

"Who wants to go to the park?" Mr. Wakefield asked after lunch the next day.

"Me, me, me!" Jessica and Elizabeth chimed in together.

Steven, who was the twins' older brother, gulped his milk. "I'm not going to the park," he said. "It's just for babies."

"It is not, Steven," Elizabeth said. "The park is for everyone. Right, Jessica?"

Jessica was glad her twin asked her what she thought. That was how it was supposed to be. She was happy to have Elizabeth all to herself again.

"I like it, too," Jessica agreed.

She opened one of her sandwich cookies and handed half to her sister. While she scraped the creme off with her teeth, she looked at Elizabeth. Elizabeth looked at her and smiled. Everything was back to normal.

In a few minutes, Jessica and Elizabeth were on their bikes. Mr. Wakefield was riding a bike, too, only his was twice as big.

"Last one to the park is a rotten egg!" Elizabeth shouted as she rode ahead.

Jessica pedaled hard to catch up. Soon she and Elizabeth were laughing and pretending to swerve into each other. When they came to the park they hopped off their bikes.

"Daddy's the rotten egg," Jessica giggled.

Their father pretended to be upset. "No

fair. I always lose." He parked his bike and went to talk to some other parents.

"Let's go to the seesaw, Jess," Elizabeth said. She started running.

Jessica stood still. She looked to see if any of their friends were in the park. She spotted lots of kids from Mrs. Becker's class, but not Eva. Jessica was glad. She ran to catch up to Elizabeth, and balanced on the other end of the seesaw.

"Do you want to do no-hands?" Jessica asked.

"OK. But no bumping."

Jessica waved her arms up and down while the seesaw tipped back and forth. "I'm a bird," she said. "I'm flying." Elizabeth laughed and waved her arms, too.

"Hey, Jessica! Look at my new bike!" Lila Fowler rode over to show off her shiny blue

bicycle. "Isn't it nice? And look, it even has a headlight."

Jessica glanced at the bicycle. "It's OK," she said without much enthusiasm. Today she wanted to play with Elizabeth only.

"Do you guys want to go on the jungle gym?" Lila asked, looking from Elizabeth to Jessica.

"Not right now," Jessica said quickly. "Maybe later."

"Well, do you want to play tag?" Lila asked. "Ken and Todd and Winston are over by the fountain. They always play tag."

"Maybe later," Jessica said again. She pushed hard off the ground and went up past Lila's head. When she came down and saw the expression on Lila's face, she added, "In a little while."

Lila was angry. "Forget it," she said and pedaled away.

"Why didn't you want to play with Lila?" Elizabeth asked. "You weren't very nice."

Jessica looked up at the sky. "No reason."

"Hey, look!" Elizabeth said suddenly. "There's Eva! Let's play with her."

Elizabeth got off the seesaw so fast that Jessica almost bumped onto the ground. With a frown, she watched her sister run over to the new girl. Then Eva and Elizabeth walked back to where Jessica was sitting on her half of the seesaw.

"Hi, Jessica," Eva said. "This is such a pretty park! I'm so happy Elizabeth told me about it."

"Liz told you?" Jessica mumbled. She rubbed her shoe in the dirt to make a pattern. All of a sudden she wasn't having any fun.

"I just got my allowance," Eva went on excitedly. "Mother says I should buy you an ice-cream cone for being my host in school."

Elizabeth smiled brightly. "Thanks!"

"And one for you, too," Eva said, looking at Jessica with a smile.

"No, thanks," Jessica said. "I have to tell Lila something important."

"OK. We'll be right back," Elizabeth said.

Jessica walked away, but she sneaked a look back over her shoulder. Eva and Elizabeth were talking and laughing while they skipped to the ice-cream stand. Jessica wondered if Elizabeth liked Eva better than her.

CHAPTER 6

I'm Mad at You!

"Twinnie! Look-alike!" Charlie Cashman yelled to Elizabeth and Jessica when they got to the bus stop on Monday. He was in their class, and he teased them all the time.

Elizabeth pretended he wasn't there. "Mrs. Becker is going to show a movie today, remember?" she told Jessica.

Jessica was fixing the laces on her sneakers. "I remember," she said in a mopey voice.

"Aren't you excited?" Elizabeth went on. She looked down at her sister. Jessica was unusually quiet, and Elizabeth was about to ask her if she was angry or sad about something when Todd Wilkins came up to her.

"Hi, Elizabeth," Todd said. He had his baseball glove and his ball with him. "Want to play catch until the bus comes?"

Elizabeth put her books down on the sidewalk. "OK. Watch my books for me, Jessica."

But Jessica just stood up and walked away. "I'll be right back, Todd," Elizabeth said as she hurried after her sister.

"Do you still feel sick?" Elizabeth asked Jessica.

"Nope." Jessica shook her head firmly.

Elizabeth was confused. "Then what—"

"The bus is coming!" Caroline Pearce yelled. "I call I'm at the front of the line."

All the older boys pushed in front of Caroline. She said the same thing every day, and

42

every day no one paid attention to her. Elizabeth ran to pick up her books.

When she got onto the bus, Jessica was already sitting with Crystal Burton, a girl in the third grade. Elizabeth took the last empty seat. She had to find out what was making Jessica so upset. Maybe she'd find out when they got to school.

"I'm going to check on Tinkerbell and Thumbelina," Jessica announced as soon as they got to their classroom. Tinkerbell and Thumbelina were the class hamsters.

"Let's go say hi to Eva first," Elizabeth said.

Jessica didn't answer. Instead she headed to the back of the room. Elizabeth watched her twin. She was very puzzled. Lila was looking in the hamster cage, too, but when she saw Jessica coming, Lila marched away.

Maybe Jessica is mad at Lila, Elizabeth thought. *Or maybe Lila is mad because Jessica didn't want to play with her yesterday.* Elizabeth couldn't figure out what was wrong.

By lunchtime, nothing had changed. Every time Elizabeth tried to ask Jessica something, Jessica pretended not to hear, or else she turned away. Elizabeth was becoming upset, too.

"Let's find a table," Elizabeth said to Eva after they had filled their lunch trays with food. She was trying to be cheerful but she didn't feel that way.

"Where should we sit?" Eva asked. "Jessica is over there." She pointed to a crowded table with a few empty seats.

Elizabeth nodded. "Come on." She spotted Amy walking that way, too.

44

"Amy's sitting here," Jessica said in a loud voice. She put her hand on the chair next to her and stared at Elizabeth. "I'm saving this seat for her."

Elizabeth's stomach flip-flopped. She didn't know what to say. She and Jessica always ate lunch together. Besides, Jessica always said Amy was too much of a tomboy. Why were they such good friends all of a sudden?

Amy sat down without saying anything to her, either. She and Jessica started whispering to each other as though no one else was around.

Eva nudged Elizabeth's elbow. "Let's go find other seats," she suggested. Her brown eyes looked huge. "They don't want us to sit with them."

"OK," Elizabeth agreed. She felt like crying. Jessica wasn't mad at Lila—Jessica was mad at her! And Amy was mad at her, too. Elizabeth didn't know what she had done. All she knew was that her two best friends were ignoring her.

CHAPTER 7

Making Hearts

The next day, Mrs. Becker announced that they would start making Valentine's Day cards.

"I'd like a volunteer to pass out the art supplies," Mrs. Becker said.

"Me, me, me!" Caroline shot her hand up. She always volunteered. "I will!" Jessica raised her hand, too.

"Jessica, how about you?" Mrs. Becker said. "And please choose someone to help you."

Jessica stood up and looked at Elizabeth.

Elizabeth looked at her hopefully. They always did things together. But Jessica looked first at Lila and then at Amy. She knew how to get back at Elizabeth for liking Eva better.

"Amy can help me," she said.

Amy jumped up with a smile. "Hooray," she cried. Lila folded her arms in anger and Elizabeth looked disappointed.

"Psst," Amy whispered when they reached the art supplies closet. Jessica took out a box of markers and leaned close to listen. "What?"

"Elizabeth was supposed to come over to my house after school," Amy said. "I want you to come over instead."

"OK," Jessica said. She grabbed some glue sticks. "But you have to tell her."

Jessica didn't really want to go to Amy's

house. She and Amy didn't like to play the same games, but she knew it was a good way to make Elizabeth feel bad for spending all her time with Eva.

"Boys and girls, spread out around the art tables," Mrs. Becker said in a loud voice. "There's plenty of room."

Jessica and Amy brought the art materials over to the large square activity table at the back of the classroom. Jessica noted that Elizabeth was sitting next to Eva. Jessica went to the opposite side and sat down next to Lila.

"I'm going over there," Lila said suddenly. She gathered her things and moved to the other table. Jessica blinked in surprise. *What a mean thing for Lila to do!* she thought.

"The first cards we make will be for our secret valentines," Mrs. Becker announced.

"I know you all have someone special you want to give a valentine to."

Jessica looked across at Elizabeth. Last year she made a secret valentine for her twin sister. But not this year! And she wasn't going to give Lila one, either.

"I know who Todd is picking!" Jerry McAllister said.

"You be quiet!" Todd shouted. His face turned bright red. He crunched up his construction paper and threw it across the table at Jerry. Then he quickly glanced at Elizabeth.

"Who are you giving yours to?" Amy asked Jessica.

Jessica thought for a moment. If she couldn't give one to Elizabeth, and she couldn't give one to Lila, who did that leave? Then she thought of someone. "Mrs. Becker,"

Jessica whispered. She began drawing a big heart.

Amy looked over at Elizabeth and frowned, "Me, too. I'm sending my secret valentine to Mrs. Becker."

Jessica didn't want Amy to copy her, but she didn't say so. "What do you want to play when we get to your house?" she asked. "Do you have a dollhouse?"

"No," Amy said. She made a face. "I have a fort outside in the bushes. We could play pirates."

Jessica crinkled her nose. Pirates! That sounded messy! She knew it was going to be a terrible afternoon. But it sure would serve Elizabeth right!

CHAPTER 8

Valentine's Day

When Elizabeth woke up on Wednesday morning, she remembered it was Valentine's Day. She looked over at Jessica's bed, but didn't feel like saying "Happy Valentine's Day" to her sister, twin or no twin.

She got out of bed and started to look for something red to wear. She was sad that Jessica and Amy had spent yesterday afternoon playing without her.

Jessica yawned sleepily, and then got out of her bed. She didn't say anything, either, until she noticed the red sweatshirt Elizabeth was putting on. "That's what I was going to wear," she said.

"So? I can wear it, too," Elizabeth answered.

The twins often wore the same outfit to school. It was fun, because then no one could tell them apart. Today, both girls half-heartedly put on their sweatshirts and their jean skirts. Both had grumpy looks on their faces as they went downstairs for breakfast.

"Happy Valentine's Day!" Mr. Wakefield said when they came into the kitchen. He gave them both a kiss.

"Happy Valentine's Day, Daddy," Elizabeth said as she kissed her father on his cheek.

"Happy Valentine's Day," Jessica said as she sat down in her chair.

Elizabeth sneaked a quick look at Jessica. Jessica peeked over at Elizabeth. Both girls looked away at the same time. It was going to be a terrible Valentine's Day.

All the way to school, Elizabeth tried to think of some way to get Jessica and Amy to like her again. But she didn't know what to do, because she didn't know why they didn't like her in the first place.

"Hi, Elizabeth," Eva said when Elizabeth got to class. "Happy Valentine's Day."

Elizabeth tried to smile. "Hi." She put her books on her desk. "It's my turn to feed the hamsters," she said. "Want to help me?"

Usually she asked Jessica or Amy to help feed the hamsters. But she couldn't ask them now.

"Sure," Eva said happily. She was silent

for a moment. "Are you sad about something?" she asked.

Elizabeth took out the hamster food. "No," she said in a very soft voice.

Together, Elizabeth and Eva looked at Tinkerbell and Thumbelina. The hamsters looked exactly alike, just like identical twins. *They* were best friends. Elizabeth sniffled.

"I'm sorry you're sad," Eva said while she put some seeds inside the cage. She sounded worried. "Are they mad at you because you like me?"

Elizabeth gulped. She didn't want Eva to feel responsible. "I don't know," she said. "I just don't understand it."

Elizabeth turned toward Jessica, who still looked grumpy. Then Elizabeth looked at Lila. Lila looked grumpy, too, and so did

Amy. No one was speaking to anyone except for Elizabeth and Eva.

Mrs. Becker placed a box on her desk, and took off the top. "I think we should begin Valentine's Day by handing out our cards," she said. She reached in and pulled one out. "The first valentine is for Julie Porter."

Julie got up to get her card. When she opened it, she smiled. "Thank you, secret valentine," she said. "Whoever you are."

Everybody giggled, except for Elizabeth, Jessica, Lila, and Amy.

"Here's one for Winston," Mrs. Becker said.

All the boys began to laugh loudly. "Woooo-oo!" Charlie shouted.

Winston turned red, but he looked happy at the same time. He read his card and then closed it. He didn't say anything, but he had a big smile on his face.

Mrs. Becker picked out another card. "Here's one for Elizabeth." She handed it to Elizabeth.

Slowly, Elizabeth opened the card. Inside was a big heart and the words, "To my secret valentine. You are a special friend."

Elizabeth glanced at Jessica who was staring at her desk. It couldn't be from Jessica. Then Elizabeth peeked over at Amy, who was staring at the ceiling. It couldn't be from Amy.

Then Elizabeth looked at Eva, who was smiling from ear to ear.

"Thanks," Elizabeth whispered with a little smile. She was glad that Eva still liked her, even though Jessica and Amy didn't.

While Mrs. Becker handed out the rest of the cards, Eva tore a piece of paper from her notebook. Elizabeth watched with curiosity while Eva wrote something on it before handing it to her.

Elizabeth opened the note. "I know why you're so sad. I have a good idea how to make everyone friends again," Eva had written.

Elizabeth looked over at Eva. "What?" she whispered.

"I'll tell you tomorrow," Eva whispered back.

Elizabeth started to feel better. She didn't know what Eva's plan was, but she wanted it to work more than anything in the world.

CHAPTER 9

All Tangled Up

The first person Jessica noticed when she got to school the next day was Eva. She looked different for some reason, but Jessica couldn't figure out why.

"Eva!" Elizabeth said. "You got some new clothes!"

That was it. Eva was wearing jeans and a knit shirt and white sneakers. She looked just like any other kid in their school now.

But something else was different about Eva, too. She had a bright smile on her face. She looked like she had a big, exciting secret that she couldn't wait to tell everyone. Jessica wanted to know what it was.

Then she remembered she wasn't supposed to like Eva.

With a big sigh, Jessica sat down in her seat between Elizabeth and Lila, and stared straight ahead. She was mad at Eva and Elizabeth for spending so much time together. She was mad at Lila for being mad at her. And she was mad at Amy for making her play pirates.

During spelling class someone tapped Jessica on the shoulder. "Psst," Ken Matthews hissed from the seat behind her.

"What?" Jessica turned around to look at him. He was holding out a note. "Who's that from?"

Ken pointed to Eva. Jessica was surprised. Why would Eva send *her* a note? She was so curious! She opened the note quickly. *Please come to the swing set at recess for a special emergency meeting,* it said.

Jessica's eyes widened. She looked over and saw Lila unfolding a note that looked the same. Elizabeth had one, too, and so did Amy! It was very mysterious!

As soon as the recess bell rang, the class raced outside. Only Jessica, Elizabeth, Lila, and Amy walked very slowly, without talking. Eva stayed behind to get something out of her bookbag.

They got to the swing set at the same time, but no one spoke. Amy was looking at a scab on her elbow. Lila was redoing the bow in her hair. Elizabeth was watching some kids play kickball. Jessica sat on the swing and stared into space.

"Hi," Eva said, running up. She was carrying a bulky paper bag. "My mother taught me a game and I need all of you to play it with me."

"Why should I?" Lila asked.

"I'll play," Elizabeth said eagerly.

"What is it?" Amy asked. Her cheeks were turning pink.

Eva took a long, looped-up string out of the bag. "Hold out your hands," she said excitedly.

Jessica didn't want to be first. She looked at Lila, and then at Amy, and then at Elizabeth. Elizabeth held her hands out. "Here," she said.

"Good," Eva said with a giggle. She began wrapping the string around Elizabeth's arms, and then wound it around her own waist once. Then, without asking, Eva began looping the string around Amy and Lila, too.

"Hey," Lila said. "What are you doing?"

Eva smiled mysteriously. "You'll see."

In a minute, Eva had tangled the long string around herself, and around Elizabeth, Amy, Lila, and Jessica. Soon they were all tied up together in one giant knot. A bunch of kids crowded around them.

"What are you doing?" Lois Waller asked. "Is it a game?"

Eva nodded. "Yes. Now we all have to get ourselves loose."

Lila and Amy started pulling their arms and legs to get away. Jessica wiggled around, too. But the more they pulled, the more they got tangled up in the strings!

"Hey," Jessica said crossly. "How are we supposed to get free?"

Eva raised her eyebrows. She smiled. "We

have to cooperate," she explained. "That the only way to do it."

"I get it!" Elizabeth shouted. "Amy, try going under this piece here." She held a piece of the string a few inches away from her arm.

Amy shrugged. "OK." She ducked under the string and that untangled her a little bit.

"Lila and Jessica should switch places," Todd said watching from the sidelines. "See how the string is crossed right there?"

Jessica didn't want to cooperate with Lila, but there was nothing else she could do.

"Look how this piece goes," Amy said. She was frowning hard in concentration. "I think Elizabeth and Eva have to hold their hands and let me step over."

Elizabeth bent her knees. She started to

giggle. Jessica didn't know what was so funny, but she soon saw how silly it was to be tangled up like a cat playing with a big ball of yarn. She looked over at Lila, and they both started to giggle, too.

"This is fun," Lila said. She smiled at Eva. "But I hope we can get out!"

Amy giggled, too. "We could be here forever!"

"We'll get out," Eva said confidently. "We can do it if we work together."

Jessica stepped through a loop of string, and ended up next to Elizabeth. Her twin looked at her. Then they both smiled.

"Are you still mad at me?" Elizabeth asked.

Jessica shook her head. "No. I'm not mad at anyone anymore."

Elizabeth leaned close to Jessica's ear.

"You like Eva, too, don't you?" she whispered.

Jessica looked at the new girl. From the very first day, Eva had been so friendly. Jessica couldn't remember why she had decided not to like her. She nodded. "Sure," she said. "But I still like you best."

CHAPTER 10

Friends Again

"Everybody into the pool!" Mrs. Wakefield called. "Last one in is a rotten egg!"

Elizabeth screamed and grabbed her shark float before jumping into the water. Four more big splashes followed as Jessica, Lila, Eva, and Amy jumped in.

"Who was the rotten egg?" Lila wanted to know.

Mrs. Wakefield was standing by the edge of the pool. "I'm not sure," she said. "It was a tie."

"We all went in at the same time!" Elizabeth agreed. "Nobody was last."

Her mother smiled. "That sounds fair. I guess you all deserve ice cream when you get out."

"HOORAY!" They all cheered at once.

Lila jumped up and down in the shallow end like a jack-in-the-box. "Let's play a game," she said. "Let's pretend we're mermaids."

"I know," Amy said. "Eva can show us how to do somersaults."

Elizabeth smiled. Being friends again was so much fun. Now everyone liked everyone else, and they had a new friend, too. Elizabeth was glad Eva had tied them up in knots!

"Meow!" came a sad sound suddenly.

Elizabeth looked over the edge of the pool. "Hey," she said to the others. "I heard a cat."

"That's what I heard last time," Eva said. "I heard a cat meowing."

The others crowded around the ladder. "Shh," Elizabeth said, putting one finger to her mouth. "Let's see if we can tell where it's coming from."

Then they all heard it again. "Meee-ow."

"I think it's in those bushes," Amy said. She began climbing out of the pool.

Jessica grabbed Amy's arm. "Don't scare it away!"

All five of the girls tiptoed over to the bushes. Elizabeth got down on her hands and knees and looked in.

"Meow!" A gray cat was hiding under the bush. It had a scratch on its ear.

"It looks lonely," Elizabeth whispered. "I wonder if it has a home."

Jessica's eyes widened. "Maybe it can live with us."

Elizabeth shook her head. "You know Steven and Dad are allergic to cats," she reminded her sister. "It makes them sneeze. We can never have one."

"But we can't just let it starve!" Jessica said.

Amy, Eva, and Lila all looked worried. The cat meowed again. It sounded just like it was crying!

Elizabeth gulped. "What are we going to do?"

Will Elizabeth and Jessica find the perfect home for the cat? Find out in Sweet Valley Kids Book #5, JESSICA'S CAT TRICK.

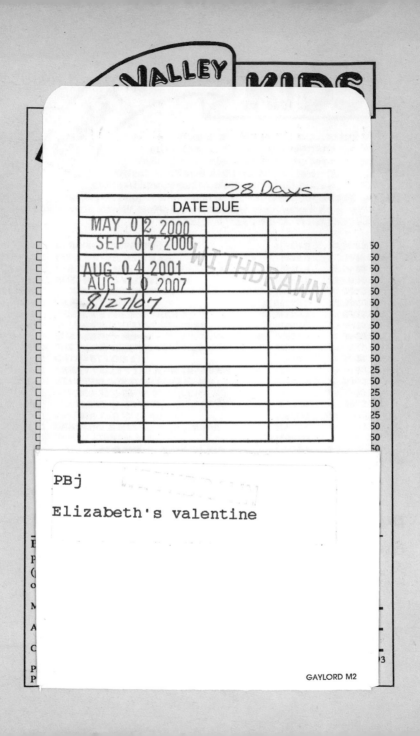

PBj

Elizabeth's valentine